The Big Hello

by JANET SCHULMAN
illustrated by LILLIAN HOBAN

Greenwillow
Read-alone

GREENWILLOW BOOKS
A Division of William Morrow & Company, Inc. / New York

Library of Congress Cataloging in Publication Data
Schulman, Janet.   The big hello.   (Greenwillow read-alone)
Summary: A little girl adjusts to her new life in California
with the help of her doll.   [1. Moving, Household—Fiction.
2. Dolls—Fiction]   I. Hoban, Lillian.   II. Title.   PZ7.S3866Bi   [E]
75-33672   ISBN 0-688-80036-X   ISBN 0-688-84036-1 lib. bdg.

To Nicole and Susi

Contents

The Trip

Don't be afraid, Sara.

Airplane trips are fun.

You are going to love
California, Sara.

Daddy says there is lots to do.

And we can play by ourselves

outside the house.

Sit back

and fasten your safety belt.

What are you crying about?

Mama says that sometimes

the air is bumpy

just like a road.

Relax.

Okay, go to sleep

and let me relax.

The New Home

See, Sara, I told you

California was great.

We have our own back yard.

We have a front yard, too.

Look at all the green grass.

Look at the clean sidewalks.

Feel the sun.

See the palm trees.

What? Don't tell me
that you like snow better.
You always cry when snow
gets into your boots.
This is a good place to live.
But I wish we had
some friends here.

Lost in California

It is not fair.

We have been in California

just two days

and Sara is lost.

How will she find
her way home?
She does not know
the policeman
on the block.
She does not know anyone.
Mama says, "Don't worry.
Sara will turn up."
But we have looked
everywhere.

I saw a big lump

at the bottom of my bed.

I thought that it was Sara hiding.

But it was just my pajamas.

I have slept with Sara

every night since I was a baby.

I will not be able

to sleep tonight.

Or tomorrow night.

Or ever.

Poor Sara.

The Dog

Hello, dog.

You do not look like Snoopy,

but I am going to call you Snoopy.

I guess that Daddy did not know

that I have always wanted

a Snoopy dog.

But you are a nice surprise.

Today was some day, Snoopy.

We had good news.

And we had bad news.

Daddy got a new job.

And I lost my old friend Sara.

You are almost as soft as Sara,

but you do not smell as nice.

And you take up

more room than Sara.

No hard feelings, Snoopy.

You are very nice.

I'll bet you are

a good hunting dog.

We can hunt for Sara tomorrow.

Good night, Snoopy.

The Big House on the Corner

Mama, guess what?

Snoopy and I found Sara!

She was on the lawn

of the big house

on the corner.

Jane was feeding her breakfast.

Oh, Mama, this is Jane.

She has been to Disneyland

five times.

But she has never been

on an airplane.

Is it okay for me to play

at Jane's house today?

I will put Sara

in my room now.

Snoopy will look after her.

They are already friends.

Friends

You sleep with me, Sara.
And you sleep
on the floor, Snoopy.
But don't be afraid.
I am right here.

Go to sleep.

We have a big day tomorrow.

Good night.